Rags the Recycled Doll

PUBLISHED BY IVY HOUSE PUBLISHING GROUP
5122 Bur Oak Circle, Raleigh, NC 27612
United States of America
919-782-0281

ISBN: 1-57197-405-9
Library of Congress Control Number: 2003096954

Printed in China

RAGS the RECYCLED DOLL

BY ANN JACKSON

ILLUSTRATED BY SHANNON O'CONNOR

Ivy House
Publishing Group

www.ivyhousebooks.com

Once upon

a time after time,

in a mixed up place

of rags and rhyme,

Lived a little girl, she was something to see.

She was made of rags, she was raggitty as can be.

All by herself she was all alone, **S**he was looking for a raggitty home.

  place

with a mending basket

and

lots of buttons

(Rags is always

losing her stuffins).

A SUNNY KITCHEN WITH LOTS OF SMELLS, EVERYONE IS FRIENDLY, AND NOBODY YELLS.

Her perfect house,

not just any house could

be it,

Rags just knew,

"I'll know it when I see it."

BUT MOST IMPORTANT   SHE HOPED TO FIND,

OFF IN A CORNER OR HIDDEN BEHIND

A DOOR, A SOFA OR ROCKING CHAIR --

A RAGGITTY FRIEND

WITH

RAGGITTY HAIR.

Somebody made
of rags,
as raggitty as can be, 
Somebody made
of rags,
recycled like me.

So she searched all over,
all up and down,
Just a raggitty little girl,
in a raggitty old town.

She wandered around
all over the place,
Looking for a smile,
or just a kind face.

She walked in the alleys,

she walked in the streets,

in search of a friend,

oh, her poor achin' feets.

t wasn't much fun,

in fact kind of ookie,

Oh, how Rags wished for a homemade CHOCOLATE CHIP COOKIE.

veryone seemed so tall
and so grim,

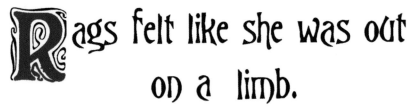ags felt like she was out
on a limb.

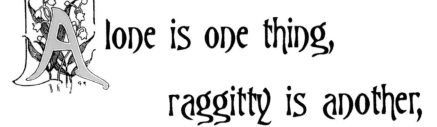lone is one thing,

raggitty is another,

but alone and raggitty ...

oh, brother.

People snubbed her and yelled,

"Rags,

You silly old thing."

It felt like her heart

was dragged 'round on a string.

Oh how she longed

for a *bed* to be made,

a *doll* of her own

and a nice neat braid.

Why the things she saw, it would make your hair curl.

Just a recycled girl, in a raggitty old world.

So she meandered around all over the city,

It wasn't easy being raggitty in a town without pity.

Oh me, oh my,
what a raggitty fate,
Always in search
of a raggitty mate.

When it came right down
to the old nitty-gritty,
Would Rags ever find a
friend in this lonely old
city?

Then one day she realized

why she had been so silly.

The answer

was right under her nose.

Yes, really!

She looked all around,
she looked near and far,

Why, she even looked
under that old pickle jar.

She looked to the left,

she looked to the right,

She looked way down deep,

dark in the night.

She searched
here and there,
she searched far and wide,
She searched
under seashells washed up
in the tide.

he had been
all mixed up
about a house and a friend,

hen all she needed at her
journey's end,

as someone to be

always steady and true.

ll this time she'd been searching,

searching for

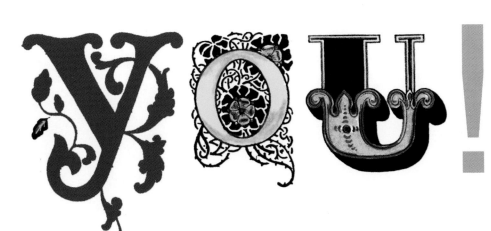

Can you find these things in the pictures?

A mouse	Cherries	A neon light
The moon	The sun	A bumblebee
A ball of yarn	Lollipops	Gumdrops
A paintbrush	A tape measure	A spool of thread
A shawl	A spider web	An apron
A mouse hole	A button box	A vase
A wind chime	A newspaper	A ship
Cowgirl boots	Stars	A bed knob
A snail	A welcome mat	Dice
A patchwork quilt	A trash can	A chimney
A checkerboard	A clock	A teacup
Polka dots	A zipper	An old jar
An old boot	An angel	A teapot
Fish bones	A rolling pin	A smokestack
Rickrack	A cloud	A seashell
A streetlight	An airplane	A skillet
A snow globe	A bow	A braided rug
A castle	A ball and jacks	Your reflection
Baby birds	An embroidery hoop	A snowflake
Bubbles	A pin cushion	A breadbox
A spy glass	Tassels	A flower pot
A hot air balloon	A newspaper stand	A tin can
A locket	A bird nest	A turtle
A lace collar	Cattails	Chocolate chips
A candy cane	Peppermint candy	A pillow
A cake plate	A rocking chair	A flower